DATE DUE

JUN - - 2013

CHARLESTON COUNTY LIBRARY

A20333 599851

CHARLESTON COUNTY LIBRARY

P9-EGM-829

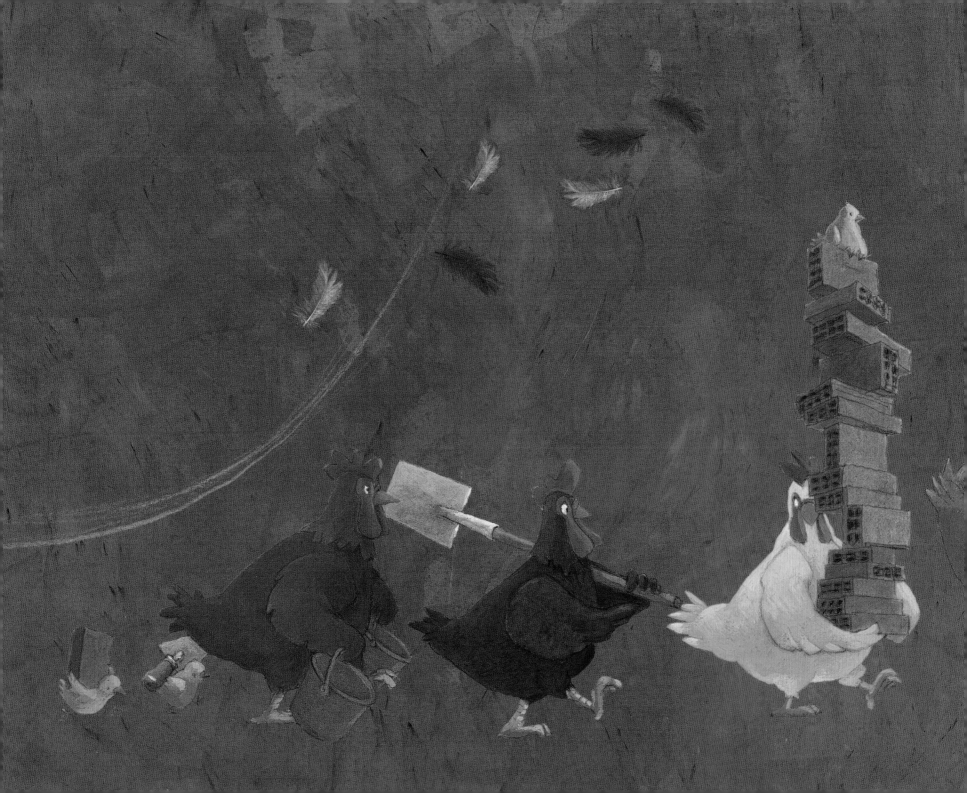

CHARLESTON COUNTY LIBRARY

THE CHICKENS BUILD A WALL

Written and illustrated by
JEAN-FRANÇOIS DUMONT

Eerdmans Books for Young Readers

Grand Rapids, Michigan • Cambridge, U.K.

On the farm, the chickens have built a wall,
though no one is exactly sure why.

It all started early one fall morning when a hedgehog showed up in the middle of the barnyard. He might have been lost, or maybe he was just looking for something to eat.

Either way, no one at the farm had ever seen a hedgehog, and everyone was fascinated by the strange new creature.

When the hedgehog saw that so many animals had gathered to look at him, he immediately curled up into a tight ball, to the astonishment of everyone in the barnyard.

The chickens clucked and the ducks quacked, and all the birds eyed the hedgehog suspiciously, but no one dared to go near him. Zita, the smallest goose, asked if maybe the new creature had just been startled by having so many animals crowd around him, but no one heard her amid all the chattering and arguing.

Edgar the rat didn't see what all the fuss was about:
"What's so interesting about this chestnut with paws?"

An old pigeon who had traveled far and wide, however,
said that he had heard about these beasts, and warned
that it was best to be cautious around them.

All this time, the hedgehog hadn't moved, and soon the birds grew tired of watching him.

They all went back to their business, though each bird still kept a wary eye on the new creature. The hedgehog stayed right where he was until night fell.

By the time the sun rose the next morning,
the hedgehog had disappeared.

In the henhouse, rumors were flying fast and furious.
"Who does that creature think he is?"
"Gone, like a thief! Strange."
"I bet he didn't leave empty-handed."
"We should count our chicks!"
"And our eggs!"

All of the birds checked on their chicks and their eggs, but none were missing. This didn't calm their fears, however.

One chicken who wanted attention declared that since the hedgehog had appeared, there were fewer worms to be found.

"It's true!" chimed in another. "The worms have gotten scarcer. I wouldn't be surprised if he ate them all."

The clucking started up again, even louder this time.

The rooster happened to be passing by just then, and decided that this was the perfect occasion to take control of a barnyard full of hens who hadn't been paying much attention to him.

"Hens, that's enough! We cannot let ourselves be tricked without doing something about it. We have to protect ourselves against prickly invaders!"

The hens quivered with excitement, carried away by the rooster's fine words. Only one little chick protested: "If we use our beaks to defend ourselves against those spikes, we'll all end up skewered!"

A shiver of fear ruffled through the hens' feathers.

"Let's build a wall around the henhouse," the rooster suggested.
"A wall so high that no wild animals will be able to get over it.
So high that even birds won't be able to fly over it!"

And all as one flock, the enthusiastic hens set to work.

To the rest of the farm, all this fuss seemed ridiculous. A mole predicted that pigs would learn to fly before the wall was finished. "You can't become a mason just like that," she added with a sniff.

Only Edgar saw an advantage. "With any luck, we won't have to hear that darn rooster crowing at dawn," he muttered, shrugging his shoulders.

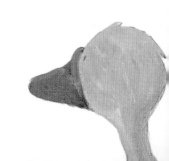

The hens ignored the mocking and kept at their work into the winter. The rooster watched over the construction and made sure that no one slacked off.

The wall grew steadily higher and higher. Soon the roof of the henhouse couldn't be seen, but the wall continued to grow.

The hens didn't even stop working when the snow began to fly. And soon the wall was taller than the barn.

But that still wasn't enough to satisfy the rooster. "The higher the wall, the safer we'll be! Keep up the good work — let's show the farm that we won't chicken out!"

Finally the wall was so high that, from the ground, no one could see where it ended.

The chickens were exhausted, and the hens had even forgotten to lay their eggs. Everyone just wanted life in the barnyard to return to normal.

They threw a huge party to celebrate the new wall, and the rooster put the last brick in place amid joyful clucking.

It was at that exact moment that the hedgehog emerged from the straw where he had spent the winter sleeping.

Since the hens had forgotten to make a door in the wall, he stayed in the barnyard waiting for the rooster to dig an opening. And since the wall was so very solid, that took all summer.

Meanwhile, the hens got used to the hedgehog. And the hedgehog wasn't afraid of the hens anymore.

And so he stayed.

© Éditions Flammarion, 2011
87, quai Panhard et Levassor – 75647 Paris Cedex 13
www.editions.flammarion.com
Originally published in French under the title *Une poule derrière un mur . . .*
by Éditions Flammarion, 2011
This English language translation © Eerdmans Books for Young Readers

All rights reserved

Published in 2013 by Eerdmans Books for Young Readers,
an imprint of Wm. B. Eerdmans Publishing Co.
2140 Oak Industrial Dr. NE
Grand Rapids, Michigan 49505
P.O. Box 163, Cambridge CB3 9PU U.K.

www.eerdmans.com/youngreaders

Manufactured at Tien Wah Press
in Malaysia in October 2012, first printing

19 18 17 16 15 14 13   9 8 7 6 5 4 3 2 1

Library of Congress Cataloging-in-Publication Data

Dumont, Jean-François, 1959- author, illustrator.
[Poule derrière un mur. English]
The chickens build a wall / by Jean-François Dumont;
illustrated by Jean François Dumont.
pages cm
Originally published in France in 2011 by Flammarion
under the title: Une poule derrière un mur.
Summary: When a friendly hedgehog visits the farm, the
chickens build an enormous wall to keep out "prickly invaders."
ISBN 978-0-8028-5422-3
[1. Toleration — Fiction. 2. Walls — Fiction. 3. Chickens — Fiction.
4. Domestic animals — Fiction.] I. Title.
PZ7.D89367Ch 2013
[E] — dc23
2012038991

FSC
www.fsc.org
MIX
Paper from
responsible sources
FSC® C012700